CHILDREN'S LITERATURE
DEPARTMENT
W9-BNO-350

Big Black Bear

Wong Herbert Yee

Houghton Mifflin Company Boston

For information about this and other Houghton Mifflin trade
and reference books and multimedia products, visit
The Bookstore at Houghton Mifflin on the World Wide Web
at http://www.hmco.com/trade/.

Manufactured in the United States of America
WOZ 10 9 8 7 6 5 4 3 2

Library of Congress Cataloging-in-Publication Data

Yee, Wong Herbert.
Big black bear / written and illustrated by Wong Herbert Yee.
p. cm.
Summary: A black bear with no manners comes to visit a little girl at home and makes a terrible mess, but another visitor helps him see the error of his ways.
ISBN 0-395-66359-8 PAP ISBN 0-395-77942-1
[1. Bears—Fiction. 2. Etiquette—Fiction. 3. Behavior—Fiction.
4. Stories in rhyme.] I. Title.
PZ8.3.Y42Bi 1993 92-40862
[E]—dc20 CIP AC

To Ellen for inspiration and exasperation.
To Mom and Dad for raising seven black bears.

Big Black Bear came out from the wood,
Stuck his nose in the air, sniffed something good!

Followed that scent from tree to tree,
Down to the City, where he shouldn't be.
Shuffling along on four furry feet
To a Brown Brick House on Sycamore Street.

Big Black Bear knocked upon the door.
Little Girl asked, "Who're you looking for?"
"I'm tired and hungry," whined Big Black Bear.
"Give me some FOOD and a Big Soft Chair!"

"Come in, please.
Wipe your paws on the mat."

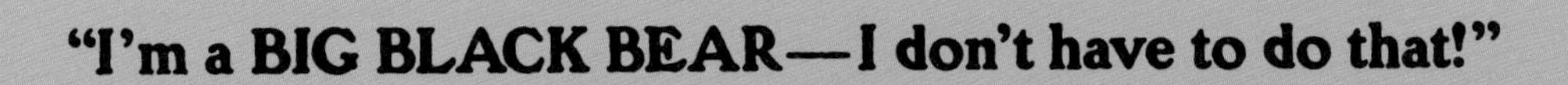

"I'm a BIG BLACK BEAR—I don't have to do that!"

He plopped in a chair, put his paws on the wall,
Leaned too far and began to fall.
Tipped the piano, came down with a "CRACK!"
Big Black Bear fell flat on his back.

"You're a **BIG BAD BEAR** with no **MANNERS** at all!"

Big Black Bear just skipped down the hall

Into the kitchen so he could try
Homemade bread and a fresh-baked pie.
Little Girl said: "Please use a dish!"
"I'm a BIG BLACK BEAR, and I do as I wish!"

He went into the pantry, but didn't get far.
Came out with his snout in a jellybean jar.
Pulled and pushed, but couldn't get it off.
Big Black Bear began to sneeze and cough.

He sneezed that jar right off his face.
Jellybeans flew all over the place.

"Cover your mouth when you cough and sneeze!"
"I'm a BIG BLACK BEAR, and I do as I please!

So, Little Girl, don't try to run away.
I'm STILL hungry and want you to STAY!

I've eaten other girls and now I'll EAT you!"

A voice cried out: "NOT a nice thing to do."

Little Girl turned and to her surprise,
In came a bear that was TWICE the size
Of Big Black Bear, now quiet as a mouse,
Hiding in a corner of the Brown Brick House.
"Little Black Bear shouldn't tell lies.
Come over here and apologize."

"I'm very sorry,
PLEASE excuse me.
I'm a Little Black Bear
who just turned three."

Little Black Bear cleaned up his mess.
Then walked on over to confess:

“I’m still hungry, MAY I PLEASE have some pie?”

"Of course you can,
and I'll tell you why.

I think you learned a lesson today—
To mind your manners when you go out to play.
And the next time you wander out from the wood.
Be sure to visit my neighborhood."